D1079480

Note to parents and carers

Read it yourself is a series of classic, traditional tales, written in a simple way to give children a confident and successful start to reading.

Each book is carefully structured to include many high-frequency words that are vital for first reading. The sentences on each page are supported closely by pictures to help with reading, and to offer lively details to talk about.

The books are graded into four levels that progressively introduce wider vocabulary and longer stories as a reader's ability grows.

Ideas for use

- Although your child will now be progressing towards silent, independent reading, let her know that your help and encouragement is always available.

- Developing readers can be concentrating so hard on the words that they sometimes don't fully grasp the meaning of what they're reading. Answering the puzzle questions on pages 46 and 47 will help with understanding.

For more information and advice, visit www.ladybird.com/readityourself

Level 4 is ideal for children who are ready to read longer stories with a wider vocabulary and are eager to start reading independently.

Special features:

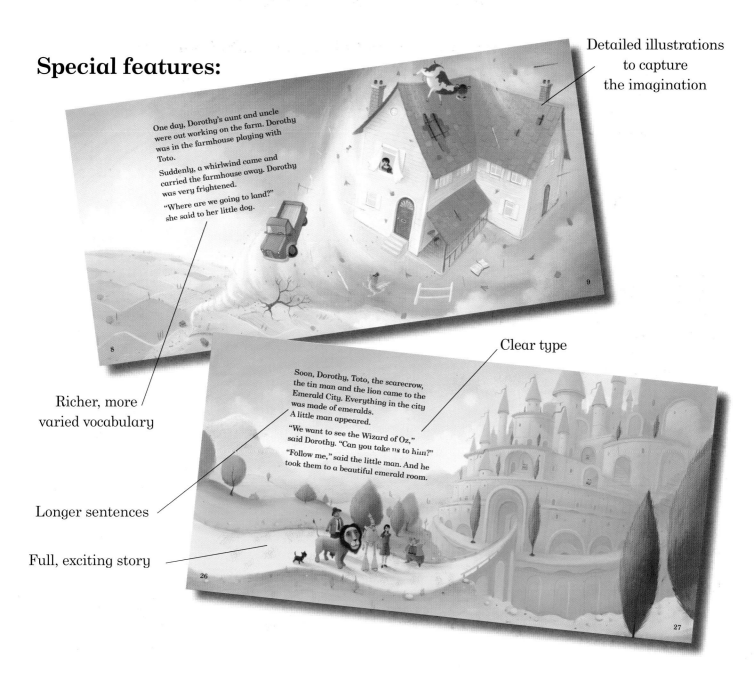

Detailed illustrations to capture the imagination

One day, Dorothy's aunt and uncle were out working on the farm. Dorothy was in the farmhouse playing with Toto.

Suddenly, a whirlwind came and carried the farmhouse away. Dorothy was very frightened.

"Where are we going to land?" she said to her little dog.

8

9

Clear type

Soon, Dorothy, Toto, the scarecrow, the tin man and the lion came to the Emerald City. Everything in the city was made of emeralds.

A little man appeared.

"We want to see the Wizard of Oz," said Dorothy. "Can you take us to him?"

"Follow me," said the little man. And he took them to a beautiful emerald room.

Richer, more varied vocabulary

Longer sentences

Full, exciting story

26

27

Educational Consultant: Geraldine Taylor

A catalogue record for this book is available from the British Library

Published by Ladybird Books Ltd
80 Strand, London, WC2R 0RL
A Penguin Company

2 4 6 8 10 9 7 5 3 1
© LADYBIRD BOOKS LTD MMX
Ladybird, Read It Yourself and the Ladybird Logo are registered or
unregistered trade marks of Ladybird Books Limited.

ISBN: 978-1-40930-366-4

Printed in China

The Wizard
of Oz

Illustrated by Richard Johnson

Once upon a time, there was a little girl called Dorothy. Dorothy lived on a farm in Kansas, America. She lived with her aunt, her uncle and her little dog, Toto.

One day, Dorothy's aunt and uncle were out working on the farm. Dorothy was in the farmhouse playing with Toto.

Suddenly, a whirlwind came and carried the farmhouse away. Dorothy was very frightened.

"Where are we going to land?" she said to her little dog.

They came down in a land full of flowers.

Suddenly, a beautiful lady appeared.

"Where am I?" said Dorothy.

"You are in the land of Oz," said the lady. "I am very pleased to see you. I am the Good Witch." She thanked Dorothy for killing the Wicked Witch.

"What Wicked Witch?" said Dorothy.

"Look under your farmhouse," said the Good Witch.

Dorothy looked under the farmhouse. There she saw a witch. On the witch's feet were two magic shoes.

Dorothy put on the shoes.

12

13

"I want to go back home," said Dorothy. "How do I get there?"

"You must go to see the Wizard of Oz," said the Good Witch. "He lives in the Emerald City, along the yellow brick road. He can help you."

"Can you come with me?" said Dorothy.

"No," said the Good Witch. "But I will be there when you need me."

So Dorothy and Toto followed the yellow brick road. Soon, they saw a scarecrow.

"Where are you going?" asked the scarecrow.

"We're going to the Emerald City, to see the Wizard of Oz," said Dorothy.

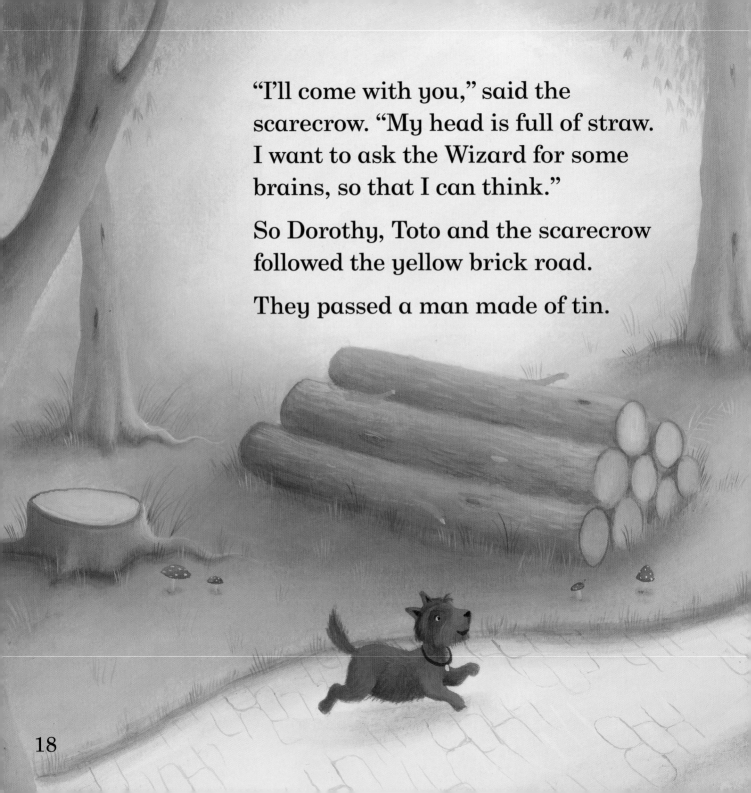

"I'll come with you," said the scarecrow. "My head is full of straw. I want to ask the Wizard for some brains, so that I can think."

So Dorothy, Toto and the scarecrow followed the yellow brick road.

They passed a man made of tin.

"Are you going to see the Wizard of Oz?" asked the tin man.

"Yes," said Dorothy.

"Can I come with you?" said the tin man. "I want to ask the Wizard for a heart, so that I can love."

So they all walked along the yellow brick road.

Suddenly, an angry lion appeared.

"Where are you all going?" asked the lion.

"We're going to the Emerald City to see the Wizard of Oz," said Dorothy.

"Can I come too?" said the lion. "I want to ask him for some courage. It's no good being a lion without courage."

Dorothy was happy with her new friends. They all followed the yellow brick road together.

24

Soon, Dorothy, Toto, the scarecrow, the tin man and the lion came to the Emerald City. Everything in the city was made of emeralds.
A little man appeared.

"We want to see the Wizard of Oz," said Dorothy. "Can you take us to him?"

"Follow me," said the little man. And he took them to a beautiful emerald room.

There they saw the Wizard of Oz.

Dorothy and her friends
were frightened.

"Wizard, can you help us?"
asked Dorothy.

"What do you want me to do?"
said the Wizard.

28

"I'd like a brain," said the scarecrow.

"I'd like a heart," said the tin man.

"And I'd like some courage," said the lion.

"And what about you?" the Wizard asked Dorothy. "What do you want?"

"I just want to go home to Kansas," said Dorothy.

"I will help you," said the Wizard. "But first, you must help me. Go and kill the last Wicked Witch in the land of Oz."

Dorothy and her friends were not very pleased. They didn't know how to kill the last Wicked Witch.

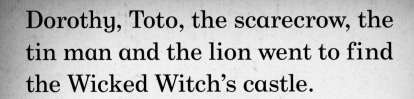

Dorothy, Toto, the scarecrow, the tin man and the lion went to find the Wicked Witch's castle.

Suddenly, the witch's flying monkeys came. They carried Dorothy, her friends and Toto back to the witch's castle.

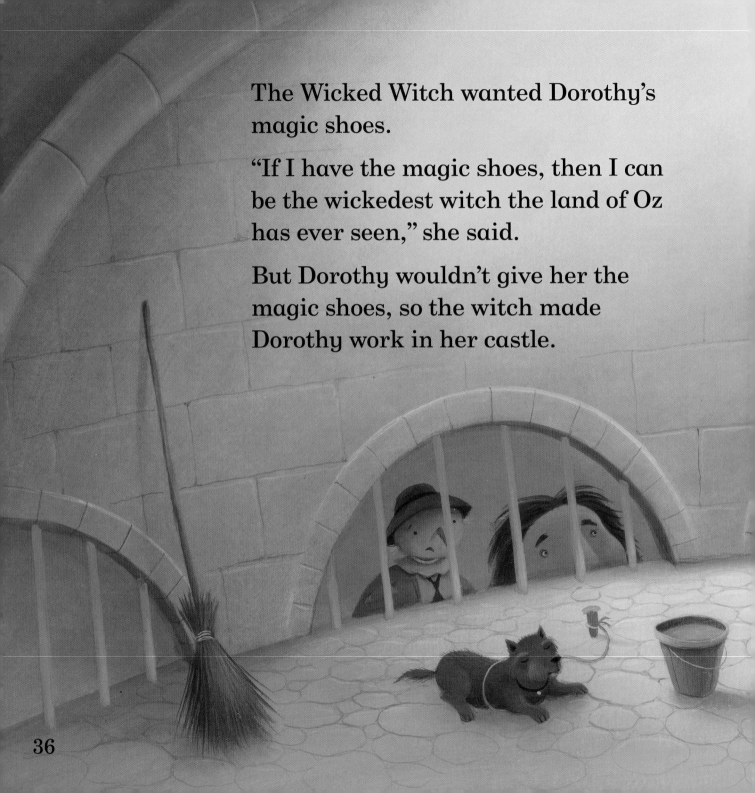

The Wicked Witch wanted Dorothy's magic shoes.

"If I have the magic shoes, then I can be the wickedest witch the land of Oz has ever seen," she said.

But Dorothy wouldn't give her the magic shoes, so the witch made Dorothy work in her castle.

One day, the witch said, "If you don't give me your magic shoes, I will kill your little dog."

Dorothy was very angry. She took a bucket of water, and threw it all over the witch.

"You wicked girl, your water is killing me," said the Wicked Witch. And she disappeared.

39

So Dorothy and her friends went back to see the Wizard of Oz.

"Now we have helped you," said Dorothy, "please will you help us?"

So the Wizard of Oz gave the scarecrow some brains, the tin man a heart, and the lion some courage.

"Now I can think," said the scarecrow.

"Now I can love," said the tin man.

"And I will be a brave lion," said the lion.

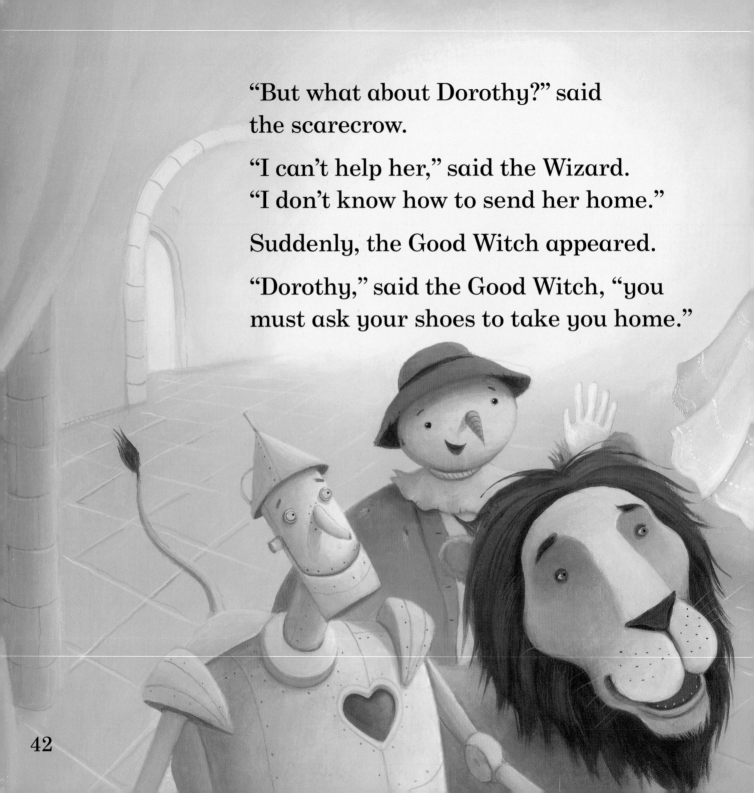

"But what about Dorothy?" said the scarecrow.

"I can't help her," said the Wizard. "I don't know how to send her home."

Suddenly, the Good Witch appeared.

"Dorothy," said the Good Witch, "you must ask your shoes to take you home."

42

"Shoes, please take me home," said Dorothy. Suddenly she was back in her farmhouse with her aunt and uncle.

And Dorothy and Toto lived happily ever after.

How much do you remember about the story of The Wizard of Oz? Answer these questions and find out!

- Who did Dorothy live with?

- What was the name of her little dog?

- Who did Dorothy meet first on the yellow brick road?

- What did the tin man want?

- How did Dorothy and her friends get to the witch's castle?

- How did Dorothy get rid of the Wicked Witch?

Unjumble these words to make words from the story, then match them to the correct pictures.

Droytoh

dizraw

crascwroe

itn amn

niol

enulc

Read it yourself
with Ladybird

The Three Billy Goats Gruff
Level 1

Cinderella
Level 1

Little Red Hen
Level 1

Goldilocks and the Three Bears
Level 1

The Magic Porridge Pot
Level 1

The Ugly Duckling
Level 1

The Gingerbread Man
Level 2

Sleeping Beauty
Level 2

Sly Fox and Red Hen
Level 2

The Three Little Pigs
Level 2

Town Mouse and Country Mouse
Level 2

Little Red Riding Hood
Level 2

The Elves and the Shoemaker
Level 3

Jack and the Beanstalk
Level 3

The Pied Piper of Hamelin
Level 4

The Wizard of Oz
Level 4

Collect all the titles in the series.